P9-CBD-608

The Ugly Duckling

Retold by
Susanna Davidson

Illustrated by
Daniel Postgate

Reading Consultant: Alison Kelly
Roehampton University

"I have six eggs," said Mother Duck.

Five eggs were smooth and small and white.

But the sixth egg was **huge**.

All spring, the mother
duck sat on her eggs,
waiting for them to hatch.
She waited...

and waited...

and waited...

One egg shell after another burst open.

"Come out! Come out!"
called Mother Duck...

...and the ducklings came
tumbling out.

They looked all around, at the tall grasses and the green leaves.

"Is everyone here?" asked Mother Duck.

But the big egg still hadn't hatched.

"Looks like a turkey egg to me," said an old duck. "I think you should leave it!"

"I'll just wait a little bit longer," said Mother Duck.

And at last, the great egg burst open.

"Cheep! Cheep!" said the duckling, looking out.

Mother Duck gasped.
The old duck spluttered.

The duckling was very large and very ugly.

"It *is* a turkey chick," said the old duck. "Take it swimming. Then you'll see."

So Mother Duck took her ducklings down to the pond. One by one, they all jumped in.

SPLASH!
Splish!
Splosh!

The dark water closed over their heads.

The next moment,
they all popped up again.

"You can swim! You're not a turkey chick," said Mother Duck.

"You're just a very ugly duckling."

Mother Duck took her ducklings to the farmyard.

The geese laughed at the Ugly Duckling and the hens pecked at it.

The turkey puffed himself up until he was red in the face. Then he gobbled at it.

The farmboy shooed the Ugly Duckling away.

He flew over the fence...

...and into a bush.

"Nobody wants me,"
said the Ugly Duckling.
"I'm too ugly."

He ran on and on.

At last he came to
a great swamp, where
the wild ducks lived.

The Ugly Duckling hid in
the swamp all night long.

In the morning, the wild ducks looked at him and laughed. "You're so ugly," they said. But then...

Gun shots flew through the air. The wild ducks took off in fright.

A great hunt was going on.

Hunting dogs splashed through the swamp.

The Ugly Duckling hid his head under his wing.

At that moment a fierce dog with glaring eyes came up to the duckling.

It stuck out its nose and showed its sharp teeth. But it didn't bite.

At last, late in the day, the gun shots stopped.

The Ugly Duckling ran out of the swamp as fast as he could.

It was so windy, he got blown this way...

...and that.

As darkness fell, the Ugly Duckling reached an old house. He crept inside.

"Can I stay here?" asked the Ugly Duckling.

"Can you lay eggs?"
asked a hen.

"No," said the Ugly
Duckling.

"Can you purr?" hissed
a cat.

"I don't think so," said
the Ugly Duckling.

"Then get out," said the cat, swiping at the duckling with its paw.

The duckling went away to a large lake.

He swam and dived every day.

But no animal would talk to him because he was so ugly.

The weather grew colder. The leaves turned yellow and brown and danced in the wind.

One evening, just as the sun was setting, a flock of birds flew across the sky.

The duckling had never seen anything so beautiful.

The birds were shining white with long, smooth necks. They were swans.

The weather grew colder and colder.

The Ugly Duckling almost froze in the ice.

But when spring came, the Ugly Duckling was still alive. He lay in the reeds and listened to the birds sing.

The Ugly Duckling raised his wings. They beat the air more strongly than before.

He flew and flew, until he came to a garden with a pond and three glorious swans.

The swans came closer, flapping their wings.

"Perhaps they'll peck me and bite me," thought the Ugly Duckling.

He bent his head to the water and saw...

...that he was no longer an ugly duckling. He was a swan!

The other swans swam around him and stroked him with their beaks.

Then a family of ducks came into the garden. They gazed at the swans.

"Look! A new one's arrived," they said.

"And he's the most beautiful one of all!"

The Ugly Duckling was first told by Hans Christian Andersen, who was born in Denmark in 1805. When he was young he was shy and awkward, but he grew up to be famous all over the world for his wonderful fairy tales.

Series editor: Lesley Sims

Designed by
Russell Punter and Louise Flutter

First published in 2006 by Usborne Publishing Ltd., Usborne House, 83-85 Saffron Hill, London EC1N 8RT, England. www.usborne.com
Copyright © 2006 Usborne Publishing Ltd.

The right of Daniel Postgate to be identified as the Illustrator of this Work has been asserted by him in accordance with the Copyright Designs and Patents Act 1988.

All rights reserved. No part of this publication may be reproduced, stored in a retrieval system or transmitted in any form or by any means, electronic, mechanical, photocopying, recording or otherwise without the prior permission of the publisher. The name Usborne and the devices are Trade Marks of Usborne Publishing Ltd.
Printed in China. UE. First published in America in 2006.

48